RUSSIAN WINTER FOLK TALES

Tatiana Sorokina

Information about Tatiana Sorokina and other books by this author, free downloads and gift ideas related to Christmas and New Year celebrations may be obtained at the author's website:
http://www.unforgettable-christmas.com

The following by Russian websites were used in creation of this book, which have wonderful collections of Russian folk tales as well as folk tales from all over the world (in Russian):
http://fairy-tales.su/
http://www.promoroz.ru/skazki/skazkidet10.php

First published by Dog Ear Publishing
4010 W. 86th Street, Ste H
Indianapolis, IN 46268
www.dogearpublishing.net

ISBN: 978-145750-595-9

This book is printed on acid-free paper.
This book is a work of fiction. Places, events, and situations in this book are purely fictional and any resemblance to actual persons, living or dead, is coincidental.

Printed in the United States of America

TABLE OF CONTENTS

INTRODUCTION

Inspired by my son, I have been dreaming about writing a children's book for a long time, and this collection of Russian folk tales about winter is a culmination of my two years of work in this field. I decided to put together this specific collection of folk tales, which I translated and adapted from Russian, because I believe it is very unique and will be appealing to all young readers and their parents for several reasons:

1. This collection includes only folk tales about **winter**. I chose this topic because there are plenty of books about Christmas, but when Christmas is over we still have more than two months of winter in store, and there is a definite gap in exciting reading material about the winter months. This is a great collection of stories to enjoy with a cup of hot chocolate next to a fireplace, but it will also inspire the readers to go outside and explore the Winter Wonderland.

2. Each folk tale I chose has an important teachable moment. I like, for example, "It was the Night Before Christmas" by C. C. Moore but, unfortunately, it lacks a basis for educational discussion between a child and a parent. All stories in my collection have a moral and a lesson to be learned. On the one hand, the stories promote such qualities as courage, friendship, hard work, generosity; on the other hand, they fight laziness, jealousy, greediness, stupidity, etc.

3. Current collections include mostly folk tales from Central Russia. But Russia stretches much further beyond its European part. Dozens of minority indigenous groups who live to the North and East of Central Russia have amazing culture and fascinating folk tales to tell, but they are hardly ever published in Russian, let alone in a foreign language. This book is an invitation to take part in an amazing journey across the whole of Russia, which is welcoming you to its magical world. Out of 20 tales included in the collection, 8 are from Northern and Eastern Russia.

4. I specifically chose folk tales that will give children answers to many burning questions they all come up with, such as, "How does winter begin? Why is the snow white? Why is the fir tree evergreen? Who is the strongest in the world?"

5. This collection of tales is very diverse. It includes stories about indigenous people, animals, fairies, and other imagined creatures so that everyone can find a story to his or her own liking.

I sincerely hope that everybody will enjoy this collection of folk tales and it will make your long, cold, winter days more fun.

ILLUSTRATIONS

This is a very special book because all illustrations in it are drawings created by the finalists of an international children's art contest, "Russian Winter Folk Tales Illustrations," that I organized in the fall of 2010. The purpose of the contest was to give children an opportunity to set their imagination free and create their own fairy tale world, not the one stereotyped and imposed on them by predominantly adult book illustrators.

More than 500 kids from ages 3 ½ to 15 from the USA, Canada, Mexico, Russia, the UK, Ireland, Romania, Greece, Turkey, China/Hong Kong, Laos, Indonesia, India, Sri Lanka, and Australia initially signed up to participate. Eventually I received about a hundred wonderful art works, each of which was unique and beautiful – I loved them all. It was the toughest job in my life to choose just one drawing per folk tale. I was amazed by the abundance of unconventional approaches and variety of styles. It was obvious that every child made a connection with the story and put a piece of his or her heart into the task, and I am deeply touched and very grateful to all of them for their efforts.

Below are the names of the artists whose drawings were included in this book, by folk tale in alphabetical order:

By Perch's Orders – Namok Eu, 15, Oxford, UK

How Fox Taught Wolf to Fish – Kathrine Veeckman, 11, Cork, Ireland

Frost – Jenna Soenksen, 12, Carlsbad CA, USA

Frost Red-Nose and Frost Blue-Nose – Anna Dmitrieva, 12, Urbana IL, USA

Hot Pancakes for Winter – Alex Gavurin, 12, Brooklyn NY, USA

How Winter Begins – Khushi Suraj, 9, India

Master of the Winds – Jacob Lokshin, 13, Reno NV, USA

The Mitten – Anastasiya Markel, 9, Paoli PA, USA

The Owl and the Raven – Audrey Zhang, 7, Levittown NY, USA

Peasant's Coat – Gieun (Jenny) Im, 15, Leonia NJ, USA

Polar Bear, Brown Bear – Devlyn Williams, 7, Houston TX, USA

Fairy Snowflake's Winter Coats – Shenali Liyanage, 10, Sri Lanka

Snowmaiden – Ilayda Celep, 11, Izmir, Turkey

Sun, Raven, and Daughter of the North – Lisa Grages, 12, Vientiane, Laos

Two Bags – Lauremy Beatriz Patual, 12, Carson City NV, USA

Two Gifts – Tiffany Walker, 13, Kapolei HI, USA

Who Is the Strongest in the World? – Jihan Az Azahra, 6, Balikapan, Indonesia

Why Snow Is White – Tatyana and Valeria Ivanova, 11, Evansville IN, USA

Why Fir Tree and Pine Tree Are Evergreen – Hoi Wah Cheng, 3 ½ Hong Kong

Winter Hut for Bull, Ram, Pig, Goose, and Rooster – Miguel Villacorta, 9, Lynnwood WA, USA

HOW WINTER BEGINS

One evening a little boy was standing near the window watching big snowflakes falling down from the sky. They were slowly dancing in the light of street lamps, and when they reached the ground they were covering everything with a thick white blanket. The snowflakes were holding hands really tight, because it was their first snow shower this year, and an unknown planet was waiting below. They didn't know what might happen down there where they had never been before. It was quiet and peaceful on the ground, and the snowflakes decided it was not all that scary.

Early in the morning, the silence came to an end. People came out of their houses and started shoveling the snow. By the looks on their faces, the snowflakes could tell that people were not very happy to see them. *It seems that we are in the way and everybody shows their discontent. This is not a very hospitable planet,* they thought. They were a little bit sad.

But soon the sun rose and started caressing the snowflakes with its golden rays, and the snowflakes cheered up and began sparkling in the sun. Maybe things were not that bad on the ground. Suddenly a group of kids showed up in the street. *Will they drive us away, too?* the snowflakes wondered. But the children were very happy to see them. They were shouting loudly, "Snow! Snow! Snow!" They were rolling in the snow on the ground and throwing the snow up in the air. The snowflakes liked the children.

One child who was covered in snow from head to toes said, "I will go ask mommy to give me my sled," and he ran toward his house.

What are 'mommy' and 'sled'? the snowflakes wondered. A nice, friendly looking woman came out of the house and gave a boy his sled and a pair of dry mittens. He laughed, then grabbed the sled and mittens, and the children started taking turns dragging each other on the sled. The snowflakes were squeaking, "Sled, sled, sled." They were happy.

On the other side of the street, two boys were playing with a small wooden shovel. One of them was taking the snow and throwing it on the other one. The boy without a shovel looked very jealous and said, "My daddy will make me a better shovel." *What is 'daddy'?* the snowflakes wondered.

Winter days are very short, and soon all the children went home. It got dark, and the snowflakes became sad again. They seemed to be especially sad because they did not know who mommy and daddy were, but they were pretty sure they lacked them. "Mommy, daddy," the snowflakes kept whispering, and the more they whispered the sadder they became, and then they started crying.

By next morning they were wet and heavy from tears, and since the sun hid behind the clouds that day, nothing would dry their tears. The children came outside again and realized that the snow was wet, and they were happier than the day before. Now they could play with snow balls and make a snowman! The children started rolling snow balls, which became bigger and bigger. *What are they doing?* the snowflakes wondered. Soon the kids stacked one snow ball on top of the other and made two snowmen. They used stones to create eyes and mouth, carrots for noses, and tree branches for arms. One snowman turned out to be bigger than the other, and the kids gave him a wooden shovel.

The snowflakes looked at the two sculptures and screamed with delight, "These are our mommy and daddy!" They laughed and sparkled and sang winter songs with the children. *It is really good here on the ground,* the snowflakes thought. They looked up at the sky and called for more of their brothers and sisters to come down and join the fun.

FAIRY SNOWFLAKE'S WINTER COATS

Snowflake is a kind and nice fairy who lives in a white castle in the whitest country in the world. This country is protected by huge mountains of cold ice. But Snowflake is not afraid of cold; her responsibility is to cover the Earth with snow every year. She has two helpers, Snow Elephant and Snow Sheep. These helpers, as all fairies' helpers, are magical animals. During spring and summer, Snow Sheep eats ice that falls from icebergs, and Snowflake uses Snow Sheep's soft fluffy wool to spin a silver yarn. Snowflake takes this yarn and 2 icicles and knits her winter coats. During summer and spring she has to knit 90 winter coats – one for every day of winter (and an extra one every 4 years for the leap year).

Snowflake puts all the finished winter coats into a beautiful box made of ice. When autumn finishes and winter comes, the fairy takes one of her winter coats and begins shaking it. The snow starts falling from the coat, and a huge snow cloud is created. Then it's time for Snow Elephant to help. To bring order to swirling snow flurries and to cover the Earth evenly with snow, he blows his trunk, and the flurries fly down to all parts of the planet in an orderly fashion. Snowflake fairy repeats her ritual every day of winter using a new winter coat. And this happens year, after year, after year…

But one year, a long time ago, winter could have been deprived of snow completely. This is how it happened. Snowflake's birthday is the last day of autumn at midnight. Usually, fairies count their years to ten, and then they stop counting because they are very busy, so they do not know if they are a hundred years old or a thousand. So that unfortunate year, an evil wizard came to Snowflake's birthday party. He was very grumpy, and he hated snow flurries because when they were dancing around they got stuck in his long beard. It really annoyed him. That's why he decided to steal Snowflake's winter coats to prevent her from shaking them and keep snow from falling.

The evil wizard had five helpers – five small evil dwarves in green coats and red shoes. He put them in his pocket and brought them to Snowflake's birthday party. He let them out of his pocket when all the guests were sitting around the table having tea and cake. Obviously, no one noticed the dwarves under the table, so they ran to the Snowflake's closet and stole the box with her winter coats. The box was big and heavy because it was made of ice, so the dwarves got very tired of carrying it. They decided not to take it all the way to the evil wizard's castle but to hide it in a crystal cave they found half-way. Then the dwarves returned to their master's pocket.

When all of the guests left, Snowflake wanted to take out a winter coat and create the first snow shower that year. She was astonished and upset when she could not find her ice box. She looked in every room of her castle, but it was gone. Then she started crying. *What will happen now?* she thought to herself. *Without my winter coats there will be no snow, the ground will be left uncovered, and all the plants will freeze. Poor plants!* She continued crying, and her tears turned into small ice balls and fell on the ground. When hail started falling instead of snow the first day of winter, all fairies and wizards realized that something was wrong. Many of them came to see Snowflake to find out what was going on. When she told them what had happened, they helped her to look for her ice box because they knew that no one else had coats like hers. But it was all in vain.

One day Wind came to visit Snowflake. He was very disturbed. "What a bad winter!" he said. "You lost your winter coats, and I cannot sing my winter song properly. I am blowing into my crystal caves, but the sound comes out wrong, as if someone tempered with one of the caves". Snow Elephant was an expert in blowing, so he suggested Wind blow really hard in that cave in order to clean it on the inside. Wind followed his advice, and everybody was surprised to see that he blew Snowflake's ice box out of the cave.

Snowflake was very happy. She immediately took one of her coats out and started shaking it. She shook the coat vigorously, and a lot of snow fell and covered all the Earth. When the snow flurries started tickling the evil wizard's beard, he understood that his trick didn't work out. So he locked himself in his castle and didn't get out the whole winter. As for Snowflake, up to this day she is still knitting her coats every summer and shaking them every winter.

WHY SNOW IS WHITE

A very long time ago, when our planet Earth didn't have any colors, there were four sisters, four great fairies who could perform wonders. Their names were Spring, Summer, Autumn, and Winter. Winter was the eldest sister, and she was the wisest. Spring was the youngest and the most energetic but a little bit light-headed. Summer was the most beautiful but a little bit lazy. Autumn was the most thoughtful and slightly sad.

One day the sisters learned from migrating birds that the Earth did not have any colors, so they decided to show their mastery and paint the planet. They gathered all their paints and brushes. Winter took a small spell book out of her pocket, read special magic words, and all four sisters were transported to Earth.

As soon as they arrived, they saw that the Earth was pale, and everything was colorless, all the trees, flowers, birds, and animals, so the fairies decided to start working immediately. Everyone worked day and night, but they could not agree what colors to use and would quarrel all the time. When Spring would paint flowers blue, Summer would come around and re-paint all flowers red.

"Why did you do that? Why did you spoil everything?" Spring would shout.

"I didn't spoil anything, I made the flowers prettier," Summer would answer.

And so they would continue arguing and shouting at each other. Then Winter would have to stop working and calm the sisters down. These arguments were taking place every single day. Autumn didn't like how Summer painted the frogs, Summer didn't like how Spring decorated apple trees blossoms, and so on and on and on…

Winter was very tired from these quarrels and was constantly looking for a way to help the sisters. Finally, she got an idea (after all, she was the wisest of all sisters and had a Magic Book). One evening, Winter gathered the fairies and asked them, "My dear sisters, aren't you tired of quarrelling?

"Oh yes, we are very tired of it!" answered Summer.

"Then I have a suggestion, said Winter. "Let's divide a year into four equal portions, and each of us will have her own time to paint Earth and other sisters will not interfere. Every one of us will do the job to our own liking, and at the end of the year we can decide which one of us was the best painter."

The sisters liked this idea very much. They divided the paints and brushers among each other and agreed on how and when they were going to take turns.

Spring was the first one to paint. She grabbed her paints and brushes and rushed away. Summer lay down under a tree to rest, Autumn sat down nearby to reflect, and Winter decided to follow Spring. Winter knew that her youngest sister was a little bit light-minded, and she wanted to make sure Spring didn't spoil anything.

Spring started her work by painting fresh new leaves on a birch tree bright green, but suddenly she saw a big butterfly and ran after her, not completing her work. Winter saw that and called to her, "Where are you going, sister? You have to finish your work." But Spring would not listen, she would only laugh and run away. Winter did not want to leave the birch tree half-painted, so she took out her own bottle of bright green paint and colored all the leaves.

In the meantime, Spring managed to catch the butterfly and paint one of her wings yellow. But at that moment she noticed a violet opening up in the grass and immediately switched her attention to the flower. Naturally, the half-painted butterfly flew away. Winter was old and could not run after the butterfly, so she waited 'til it sat on a tree and then finished the job. The butterfly turned out to be beautiful bright yellow.

All during the Spring's time, Winter was looking after her youngest sister and got very tired. But she was happy, because next was Summer's turn. Summer was never rushed, and she would never run around like Spring did. When Summer's time came, she started working very thoroughly. She never missed a leaf or a flower, but she got exhausted quickly and lay down to rest. While Summer was sleeping, several ducklings hatched near a pond. Winter noticed the ducklings, and she was afraid they would get lost because they were colorless. So she tried to wake Summer up, but it was impossible, as she turned from one side to the other and continued sleeping. Winter pitied the ducklings and painted them herself with her own paints.

Later on Summer woke up, worked a little bit more, and hid under a tree again because she was too hot. Winter tried to persuade her to come out of the shade and keep working, but Summer did not move a finger. Winter knew that there was no time to lose. Berries and mushrooms started appearing in the forest, so Winter took her bag of paints and brushes and went on painting day and night.

Soon Summer's time was over, and Autumn took her turn. Winter was sure that thoughtful Autumn would do her job properly. Finally, Winter hoped to have a chance to sit down, relax, and read a book. She was thinking about her cozy armchair when she suddenly heard her three sisters arguing again. Spring and Summer were yelling, and Autumn was crying.

"What happened?" Winter asked.

"We used such beautiful shades of green to color the leaves and grass, but stupid Autumn is coloring them yellow and red now. She is ruining our work." Spring and Summer complained.

Autumn started sobbing and even bigger tears were running down her cheeks. Winter could not stand this injustice and became very angry. "Did you forget our agreement, sisters? Autumn did not interfere with your work when you were painting; now let her do what she wants. If you do not stop quarrelling, I will send you back home right away, and I will never let you color the Earth!" Winter's eyes looked fierce, and it was clear she was not joking.

Spring and Summer became terrified of their eldest sister's anger. They also realized that they were wrong and unfair towards Autumn and apologized to her, but poor Autumn kept crying. "They broke all the jars of my favorite paints, and now I have nothing to paint with!" Winter smiled, hugged Autumn and gave the golden-haired sister her own jars of yellow, orange, red, and brown paints.

When Winter's turn came to paint, she realized that she only had white color remaining, since she had already used all the others. Colorless snow started falling from the sky, covering the fields, meadows, and forests. There was so much of it that Winter quickly decided to take her biggest brush and paint it white. Then she took out a small brush and started drawing exquisite snowflakes and wonderful frosted motifs on the windows of people's houses. She also made rabbits and polar bears white and continued working tirelessly. The other three sisters were very surprised to see that Winter didn't use any other colors but white. Then they figured out what had happened. So they gathered all the paints they had remaining and brought them to Winter.

"Dear Winter, please, take our paints," they said. "You were so kind to us and taught us so much."

Winter was very happy to see that her sisters learned a lesson. She used some of the paints to color animals' and birds' eyes, noses, and beaks, and then she took all the bright colors and painted decorations on a New Year tree[1]. They were so beautiful and colorful that the other sisters stood looking at it in awe, and then all three of them said together, "You, Winter, are the best painting master of all!"

Everybody started dancing around the New Year tree. Both kids and grown-ups were laughing and singing because the New Year celebration turned out to be so bright. Winter was standing nearby wishing every one Merry Christmas and Happy New Year. All people, animals, and fairies were very happy, and no one was upset that the snow was just plain white.

---

[1] "New Year tree" is the name of the Christmas tree in Russia.

FROST RED-NOSE AND FROST BLUE-NOSE

Once upon a time, two brothers, Frost Red-Nose and Frost Blue-Nose, went for a walk in the countryside on a cold winter night. They walked in the fields and played in the forest, jumping from a tree branch to a tree branch, and they skated along frozen rivers. The moon was shining brightly, and as far as the brothers could see, there was not a soul outside. All villagers stayed home.

"Look brother, there is no one outside. Everybody is afraid to go out in such cold weather, this is our kingdom!" Frost Blue-Nose said.

"If anyone dares to show his nose outside, we will freeze him and turn him into an ice sculpture," Frost Red-Nose answered.

When morning came and the sun rose, the villagers, most of whom were farmers, came out of their houses to do their everyday jobs. The two brothers were very surprised and angry that people were not afraid of the Frosts, so they decided to teach them a lesson.

"Brother, I have noticed that two farmers ventured far away from the village. The one with a new sleigh full of goods and a fast horse is going to the market to sell his produce. I think he is a rich guy. The other one, poor fellow, has an old sleigh and is probably going to the forest to cut wood. Let's follow them and scare them to death," Frost Red-Nose suggested.

"Let's do it, brother!" Frost Blue-Nose agreed. "I will go after the rich guy, and you will follow the poor one – let's make it a competition and see who can freeze a man first."

And so the two Frost brothers ran in different directions. Frost Blue-Nose had to run for a long time. The rich farmer's horse was really good and fast, but eventually the Frost caught up with him. He climbed under the farmer's fur coat and started to destroy the warmth from underneath. The farmer started to feel the cold and raised the collar, pulled down his fur hat, and tied his warm woolen scarf tighter, but nothing helped. He even tried to make his horse go faster, but that didn't work, either. He was freezing, and even his nose turned blue. Frost Blue-Nose was laughing – it only took him 10 minutes to do the job.

Meanwhile, Frost Red-Nose caught up with the poor farmer. *His coat is thin and old,* thought Frost Red-Nose. *It will take me not more than 5 minutes to freeze this guy.* So he climbed under the poor farmer's coat and started to destroy the warmth.

The farmer felt the cold and said to himself, *Hey, it's getting colder. I have to do something about it.* He got off the sleigh and started walking, and then running, next to his horse. After half a mile, he got really hot, got back into his sleigh, and continued riding without any problem.

Frost Red-Nose was really upset. "All right, you win this time", Frost Red-Nose said, "but I will wait for you in the forest and teach you a lesson."

When the poor farmer arrived in the forest, he took his axe and started chucking the wood. He worked really hard and got so hot that he even had to take off his coat. His cheeks were red, his eyes were bright, and he looked very healthy.

"Aha!" laughed Frost Red-Nose. "I could not freeze you when you were riding or chucking the wood, but now I will get into your coat and turn it to ice. Let's see what you are going to do then." He climbed into the coat, and it turned white as snow.

When the poor farmer finished his job and loaded his sleigh with the wood, he turned to pick up his coat and noticed that it was all frozen. "Now, look who is here! I think it is Brother Frost." said the farmer. "I will have to break the ice to be able to put my coat back on." He took his whip and started hitting the coat really hard. Frost Red-Nose screamed, jumped out of the coat and ran away.

When the Frost Brothers met later in the field, Frost Blue-Nose boasted, "I froze that rich farmer in just 10 minutes! What about you, brother?"

"I failed to freeze this poor guy, brother," answered Frost Red-Nose. "He has some magic powers…"

WINTER HUT FOR BULL, RAM, PIG, GOOSE, AND ROOSTER

An old peasant and his wife had a bull, ram, pig, goose, and rooster. One day the peasant told his wife, "Our rooster is useless, let's make a holiday dinner out of him."

"All right, let's do it", his wife answered.

The rooster overheard their conversation, got scared, and ran away to the woods. When the man went looking for the rooster, he couldn't find him, so he told his wife, "The rooster disappeared, let's eat the pig."

"Fine, let's eat the pig," his wife agreed.

The pig heard that, got frightened, and ran away to the woods, too.

When the old peasant couldn't find the pig, either, he suggested they bake a goose, and his wife didn't mind. The goose heard that and told the ram, "Now they want to bake me, you will be next. Let's run away together."

So that same night they both left the house. The bull decided not to wait for what fate had in store for him and followed the two.

It was summer, and the fugitives enjoyed their life in the woods. It was warm, and there was plenty of food. But soon autumn came, and winter was approaching. One day the bull came to the ram and said, "Winter is coming, we need to build a hut to protect us during the cold months."

"I don't want to build a hut," the ram answered. "I have a warm fur coat, I am not afraid of cold."

Then the bull went to talk to the pig. "Winter is coming, we need to build a hut."

"I don't need a hut. I will dig a den in the ground and live there," the pig replied.

So the bull went to talk to the goose. "It will be very cold soon, we need to build a hut."

"I don't need a hut. I will lie on one wing and cover myself with the other, and I won't get cold," the goose answered.

Finally, the bull approached the rooster with the same suggestion. "Winter is coming, we need to build a hut."

"I don't need a hut," the rooster replied. "I will live under a fir tree, it will protect me from snow and cold weather."

The bull had nothing left to do but to build the hut alone. He worked hard, and the wooden hut he built was very nice and warm. Winter that year turned out to be especially cold. The ram was running all day but could not warm himself up, so he decided to go to the bull's hut.

"Ba-ba, bull, please let me in," he asked.

"Go away! You said you had a warm fur coat, and you don't need the hut," the bull answered.

"If you don't let me in, I will break the door with my horns, and you will freeze, too," threatened the ram. The bull didn't want his door broken, so he let the ram in.

Soon the pig, who didn't manage to dig a den in the frozen ground, showed up on the doorstep. "Oink oink, bull, please let me in," he said.

"Go away! You said you would dig a den for yourself, and you don't need a hut," the bull answered.

"If you don't let me in, I will start digging at the corners of your hut, and soon it will collapse," the pig said. The bull didn't want the pig to destroy the hut, so he let him in.

Meanwhile, the goose came to the hut, too, because he couldn't warm himself up with his wings. "Ga-ga, bull, please let me in," he said.

"Go away! You said you didn't need a hut because you had two wings to cover yourself," the bull answered.

"If you don't let me in, I will pick out all the moss you used for insulation between the logs, and you will freeze, too," said the goose. The bull didn't want the goose to pick out all the insulation, so he let him in.

Finally, when the rooster realized that the fir tree branches would not warm him up, he came to the bull's hut. "Cock-a-doodle-doo, bull, please let me in," he said.

"Go away! You said you didn't need a hut because a fir tree would protect you from the cold," the bull replied.

"If you don't let me in, I will get to the attic and sweep away all the dirt you used for insulation of your roof, and you will freeze, too."

The bull gave up and let the rooster in. They were all living together for some time when one day a hungry bear and a hungry wolf were passing by. They noticed a hut in the woods. The smell coming out of the hut was very delicious.

"Let's burst in and eat everybody," suggested the wolf.

"Let's do it!" the bear agreed. "But you go in first, you are faster and more resourceful than I am."

So the wolf ran to the hut, opened the door, and jumped inside. The bull was the first one to see the intruder. He rushed to the wolf and nailed him to the wall with his horns. Then the ram ran towards them and started beating the wolf with his horns. The goose was also helping as much as he could, he was pinching the wolf with his beak. The rooster wanted to scare the wolf too, so he started running up and down the room yelling, "Give him to me! I have a knife, he won't leave alive!" And the pig, who was in the basement at the time, decided to frighten the wolf by shouting, "I am sharpening axes and knives, I want to eat the wolf alive!"

When the bear heard the frightful sounds coming out of the hut, he decided not to risk his life and hid in the bushes near the hut while waiting for the wolf to finish his job. In a few minutes, the wolf ran out of the hut, screaming. The bear followed him, and he managed to catch up with him only far away from the hut near a forest lake.

"What happened there?" the bear asked the wolf.

"It was horrible," the wolf answered, "they nearly beat me to death. First, a huge guy in a black coat ran towards me and nailed me to the wall with an oven fork. Then a medium-size guy in a white coat started beating me with a butt. Then a small guy in a grey coat began pinching me with tweezers. Meanwhile, the smallest guy in a red robe was running up and down the room yelling, "Give him to me! I have a knife, he won't leave alive!" And on top of that, someone in the basement was shouting continuously, "I am sharpening axes and knives, I want to eat the wolf alive!"

After that, the bear and the wolf never approached the hut again, and the bull, ram, pig, goose, and rooster lived happily ever after.

HOW FOX TAUGHT WOLF TO FISH

Once upon a time, there was an old man who lived with his wife. One winter day he told her, "You bake pies, and I will take the sled and go fishing."

He thought it was his lucky day, he got the whole sled full of fish. Little did he know that a fox was following him and saw his great catch. The fox immediately came up with a plan for how to get hold of all the fish. She lay in the middle of the road leading from the river to the village, pretending to be dead.

On his way home, the old man saw the fox and stopped his sled. *What a great find!* he thought. *It will make a wonderful collar for my wife's winter coat.* The old man picked up the fox and put it in the sled.

All the way home, the old man didn't look back. Meanwhile, the fox opened her eyes and started carefully throwing fish off the sled on the road, one by one. She threw off all the fish and left unnoticed, herself.

When the old man came home he told his wife, "I brought you a nice fur collar for your winter coat." The old woman searched the sled but couldn't find either the fur or the fish. She was very angry, and she scolded her husband. Only then he realized that the fox was alive. He was upset, but there was nothing he could do about it.

In the meantime, the fox gathered all the fish in one pile and was having a nice lunch. A wolf was passing by and said, "Hello, fox. I salute you!"

"You may salute as much as you want, but keep away from my lunch."

"Give me some fish, please."

"Catch it yourself and eat."

"I cannot fish…"

"This is not a big deal. I managed to do it. You will be able to do it, too. I will teach you. Go to the river, put your tail in an ice-hole, and chant, `Big fish, small fish come to me! Big fish, small fish come to me!' The fish will jump on your tail. The longer you sit, the more you catch."

The wolf went to the river, put his tail in an ice-hole, and started chanting, "Big fish, small fish come to me! Big fish, small fish come to me!"

The fox followed him, and while she was wandering nearby, she was chanting, "The stars in the sky are shining, the wolf's tail is freezing!"

The wolf heard her murmuring something and asked, "What are you whispering?"

"I am just herding fish towards your tail, "answered the fox and then again said to herself, *The stars in the sky are shining, the wolf's tail is freezing!*

The wolf spent the whole night near the ice-hole, so his tail froze in it. In the morning. he wanted to stand up he couldn't. *I probably have so many fish on my tail that I cannot even lift it,* he thought.

At that time a woman from the village came to the river to get water. She saw the wolf and started screaming, "Help, help! There is a wolf here! Beat him, beat him!"

The wolf tried to move forward and backward but could not release his tail. The woman dropped her water buckets and started hitting him with a yoke.[2] The wolf pulled really hard, tore off his tail, and ran away. *All right, slimy fox. I will pay you back,* he thought.

Meanwhile, the fox got into that woman's house, ate almost all the fresh dough, and used a little portion of it to cover her forehead. Then she ran outside, fell on the ground, and started moaning. The wolf saw her and said angrily, "This is how you teach fishing?! Look, I was beaten all over…"

The fox answered, "Oh, my friend, you are missing a tail, but at least your head is intact. Look, people broke my head, and my brain is flowing out. I can hardly move…"

"That's true," the wolf said. "How could you walk by yourself? Climb on my back, I will carry you."

The fox climbed on the wolf's back, and he carried her home. While he was walking, she was singing, "The injured is carrying the uninjured, the injured is carrying the uninjured."

"What are you saying?" the wolf asked.

"I am just trying to magic away your pain," the fox replied and then continued to herself, *The injured is carrying the uninjured, the injured is carrying the uninjured…*

---

[2] Yoke = "a shaped wooden beam used across a person's shoulders to carry a pair of items (such as two pails of milk or water), by hanging one from each end (Wikipedia).

FROST

Once upon a time, there was an old man who had a daughter. His first wife died, and he married a woman who had a daughter of her own. It was very hard for the old man's daughter to live with a stepmother. The stepdaughter was always at fault, and the woman's own daughter was always right. The stepdaughter did all the work about the house. She fed farm animals, brought water from the river, chopped up firewood, and cleaned the house, but the stepmother was never happy.

One day the old woman decided to get rid of her stepdaughter and ordered her husband, the girl's father, "Take her away from here, I cannot stand her any more! Take her to the woods and leave her there."

The old man cried for a while, but he couldn't argue with the old woman. So he harnessed his horse and asked his daughter to sit in the sleigh. He took the girl to the forest and left her there under a big fir tree. It was a very cold winter, and the girl was shivering from cold when suddenly she heard Frost walking on top of the trees, "Crack-crack-crack…" When he reached the fir tree under which the girl was sitting, he looked down at her and asked, "Are you warm enough, young lady?"

She answered, "I am warm, Frost. I am warm, Master of the Winter."

Frost got a little bit down from the top of the tree; he started freezing more and asked, "Are you warm, my dear? Are you warm, my beautiful?"

The girl was barely breathing, but still she answered, "I am warm, Frost, your Highness. I am warm."

Frost got even lower and started freezing even more and then asked again, "Are you warm, my girl? Are you warm, my darling?"

The girl was hardly moving her tongue, but still she said, "I am warm, your Majesty."

Frost took pity on her and warmed her up with fur coats and down-filled blankets.

Meanwhile, the stepmother was baking pancakes and giving a wake for her stepdaughter. She told her husband, "Go to the forest, bring your daughter's body – we will bury her."

The old man jumped into his sleigh and rushed to the forest. When he approached the big fir tree, he was astonished to see that his daughter was sitting under the tree very happy and healthy in an exquisite arctic fox fur coat, with gold and silver jewelry and a huge box full of expensive gifts next to her. The old man put all the riches in his sleigh and drove his daughter home.

At home, the stepmother was baking pancakes, and the dog was barking under the table, "Bow-wow, the old man's daughter is coming with gold and silver, and the old woman's daughter will never marry."

The stepmother threw the dog a pancake and said, "You are saying it wrong. You should say it like this, 'The old woman's daughter has plenty of grooms, and the old man's daughter has only bones.'"

The dog ate the pancake but still barked, "Bow-wow, the old man's daughter is coming with gold and silver, and the old woman's daughter will never marry."

The stepmother threw the dog more pancakes and tried beating it, too, but the dog still insisted on the story. Suddenly the old woman heard the gate opening. She ran outside and was bewildered to see her stepdaughter healthy and sound in gold and silver jewelry and with a huge box of gifts next to her in the sleigh.

The old woman rushed back into the house and told her own daughter to get dressed quickly. Then she ordered her husband, "Take my daughter to the forest and leave her on the same spot where you left yours!"

The old man took his wife's daughter to the forest and left her under the same big fir tree. The old woman's daughter was sitting there shivering from cold, but not for too long. Soon she heard Frost walking on top of the trees, "Crack-crack-crack…" When Frost saw her, he asked, "Are you warm enough, young lady?"

She answered to him, "I am very cold. Don't crack around here, Frost!"

Frost got a little bit down from the top of the tree; he started freezing more and asked, "Are you warm, my dear? Are you warm, my beautiful?"

"My hands and feet don't feel anything from cold. Go away, Frost!"

Frost got even lower and started freezing even more and then asked again, "Are you warm. my girl? Are you warm, my darling?"

"I am frozen to the bone. Get lost, stupid Frost!"

Frost got angry and froze her to death.

The next morning, the old woman was scolding her husband again. "What are you still doing here? Go to the forest to pick up my daughter."

The old man left, and the dog under the table started barking, "Bow-wow, the old man's daughter is going to be married, and the old woman's daughter is going to be buried."

The old woman shouted at the dog, "You are saying it wrong! You should say, 'The old woman's daughter is coming with gold and silver…'"

But the dog insisted. "Bow-wow, the old man's daughter is going to be married, and the old woman's daughter is going to be buried."

Suddenly the old woman noticed the sleigh approaching. She ran outside and saw her daughter's body in it. She started crying, but it was too late…"

PEASANT'S COAT

One very cold winter day, a peasant went to the forest to chuck firewood. It was freezing outside, but he worked so hard that he got really hot so that sweat beads showed on his forehead. He took his coat off, put it on a tree stump, and continued working.

A rich man was passing by in his sleigh and saw the peasant. He stopped and asked him, "Hey, poor man, I am freezing here in my fur coat and you have sweat beads on your forehead. What's your secret?"

The peasant answered, "Your fur coat is no good. I have a magical coat. It lies here on a tree stump and creates heat waves. That's why I am hot."

The rich man said, "Let's trade! I will give you my fur coat, and you will give me your coat."

The peasant replied, "It's not a fair trade. My coat looks old and thin, but it is *magical…*"

The rich man asked, "How much money do you want on top of the fur coat?"

"Fifty rubles."

The rich man gave the poor man 50 rubles and his fur coat, put on the peasant's coat, and left. The poor man put on the fur coat and went home, too. The rich man didn't ride a mile when he got frozen to the bone. The whole winter he was cursing the peasant, and the peasant was laughing and showing off his new coat.

THE MITTEN

One winter day an old man was walking in the woods with his dog and dropped a mitten. A mouse was passing by and found the mitten. It was warm inside, so she climbed in and said, "I will live here."

Soon a frog stopped by and asked, "Who lives in this mitten?"

"I am a mouse in a grey blouse. Who are you?"

"I am a frog in green clogs[3]. Please, let me in."

"Please, come in."

So the two of them started living together. Then a hare was running nearby and saw the mitten. He asked, "Who lives in the mitten?"

"We are a mouse in a grey blouse and a frog in green clogs. Who are you?"

"I am a hare with a fair hair. Please, let me in."

"Please, come in."

Now there were three of them. A fox was passing by and asked, "Who lives in a mitten?"

"We are a mouse in a grey blouse, a frog in green clogs, and a hare with a fair hair. Who are you?"

"I am a fox in red socks. Please, let me in."

"All right, come in.

The four of them continued living in the mitten. Later a wolf stopped by and asked, ""Who lives in the mitten?"

"We are a mouse in a grey blouse, a frog in green clogs, a hare with a fair hair, and a fox in red socks. Who are you?"

"I am a wolf in a blue scarf. Please, let me in."

"All right, come in."

The wolf got in, and so they were five all together. Not too long after that, a boar came to the mitten and asked, ""Who lives in a mitten?"

"We are a mouse in a grey blouse, a frog in green clogs, a hare with a fair hair, a fox in red socks, and a wolf in a blue scarf. Who are you?"

"I am a wild boar at your door. Please, let me in."

It started to be a problem when everyone wanted to get into the mitten.

"You fill not fit in."

"I will try to fit in somehow, please let me in!"

"Well, what can we do with you? Climb in."

The boar squeezed in, and the six of them felt really tight – no one could move a limb. At that moment a bear showed up and asked, ""Who lives in a mitten?"

"We are a mouse in a grey blouse, a frog in green clogs, a hare with a fair hair, a fox in red socks, a wolf in a blue scarf, and a wild boar. Who are you?"

---

[3] Clogs – shoes with a wooden sole.

"Oh, there is a whole bunch of you here. I am a bear in brown outwear. Please, let me in, too."

"How can we let you in? We can barely breathe in here."

"Please, let me stay with you somehow!"

"All right, stay here by the doorstep."

The bear climbed in, and so they were now seven in total. The mitten could not be any tighter. It felt like it was going to be torn at the seams.

Meanwhile, the old man noticed that one mitten was missing, so he went back to the forest to look for it. His dog accompanied him. It was sniffing under every bush, trying to help the old man find his mitten, and suddenly it caught sight of the mitten under a fir tree. It started barking loudly, and the animals got scared, jumped out of the mitten, and ran away. The old man picked up the mitten and went home.

Snowmaiden

Once upon a time, there was an old man, Ivan, who lived with his wife, Marya. They lived a long and happy life together in a small village, and there was only one problem: they could not have children. They were very upset and disappointed because they loved kids very much. They only found consolation in looking at neighbors' kids. Eventually they resigned to their fate and kept living, just the two of them together.

One winter there was a heavy snow fall. Snowdrifts were knee-high. All children in the village were very excited. They ran outside and started playing, making snow forts and snowmen. Ivan and Marya sat in the kitchen by the window observing the children play when suddenly Ivan suggested, "Let's go outside and make a snowman, too."

"Well," Marya said, "let's go have some fun! Why do you need a snowman though? Let's make a kid from snow since God did not give us one."

"That's a good point...," Ivan said. He took his hat, and they went outside. They worked thoroughly and made a nice snow sculpture with legs, arms, and a head.

A neighbor who was passing by asked them, "What are you making?"

"Can't you see?" Ivan said.

"Snowmaiden..." Marya answered, laughing.

Ivan wanted to add some nice touches to the snow girl, such as eyes, a nose, and a mouth. When he was finishing making the mouth, he suddenly felt warm breath. He got scared and took his hand away. He looked at the Snowmaiden and noticed that her eyes had turned blue and her lips were turning pink that very moment.

What is happening? Is it an apparition? Ivan wondered and made the sign of the cross.

Meanwhile, the girl started to turn her head and move her legs and arms in the snow.

"Oh, Ivan, Ivan!" Marya cried with delight. "This is God giving us a child!" She hugged Snowmaiden, and the snow fell off her like an egg shell from an egg, and she turned into a real girl.

"Ah, my dear Snowmaiden, my darling," the old woman whispered and led the girl inside their house. Ivan could hardly believe such a miracle, and Marya was beyond herself with joy.

Snowmaiden was growing strong and healthy, which made the old couple very happy. All the girls started gathering in their house. They loved playing with Snowmaiden, dressing her up, singing songs, and teaching her everything they knew. Snowmaiden was a smart girl and a quick learner, and she easily absorbed new things, copying the other girls.

During the winter Snowmaiden grew to look like a girl age thirteen or so. She talked well in a sweet voice and understood everything she was told. She was kind, nice, and obedient. She had blue eyes like forget-me-nots and waist-long, straw colored hair, which she used to make into a braid. The only thing she lacked was the glow on her cheeks, as if she didn't have any blood at all. But even without the glow, she was very pretty. Snowmaiden was a pleasure to talk to and fun to play with, and Marya and Ivan loved her dearly.

"See, Ivan," the old woman would say. "In the end, God gave us happiness. Our days of misery are over."

The old man would answer, "Thanks, God! Nothing is forever, neither happiness nor sorrow."

Winter passed and spring came. The sun was shining bright, the first grass appeared in the meadows, and birds were returning from the South. All the young girls were happily playing outside. But Snowmaiden turned gloomy.

"What's happening, my child?" Marya used to say while embracing her. "You are not sick, are you? You do not look happy any more, and you seem to be a little thinner… Did anyone put an evil eye on you?"

Snowmaiden would answer, "Don't worry, Grandma. I am healthy…"

Soon all the snow melted, trees started to bloom, and nightingales began singing their songs. Nature was full of life, but Snowmaiden became even more miserable. She avoided playing with her friends and tried to always hide in the shade away from the sun. The only thing she loved doing was playing in a cold stream in the forest.

Snowmaiden enjoyed the shade and cool weather, and rain was her favorite. When it was dark and rainy, she was happier. Once a big black cloud brought the hail. Snowmaiden was as excited as if she was given expensive pearls. When the sun came out and the hail melted, Snowmaiden cried her eyes out as if she herself wanted to turn into watery tears. She looked like a sister crying over her dead brother…

Time flew and summer came eventually. Villagers were preparing to celebrate Ivan Kupala day[4] and Snowmaiden's friends were going to the forest for the feast, too. They stopped by Ivan and Marya's house and asked to let Snowmaiden join them. Marya was reluctant to let her go, and Snowmaiden was not very enthusiastic either, but her friends insisted she would have fun, and finally she agreed to follow them. Before they left, Marya told the girls, "Keep an eye on my Snowmaiden. She is the most important thing in my life."

"We will, don't worry!" the girls answered and rushed away.

In the forest the girls made flower wreaths and sang songs. When the sun set they put on their wreaths, made a bonfire from small branches and grass, and started jumping over it one by one. Snowmaiden was the last in the queue.

"Look," the girls told Snowmaiden, "you run when we run and then jump, don't fall behind!"

Everyone were singing and running when they heard something hissing and a plaintive scream, "Ah!"

The girls stopped, frightened. They looked around but there was nothing scary in sight except that Snowmaiden was not with them anymore. *She must be playing hide-and-seek*, the

---

[4] Ivan Kupala day – feast of St. John the Baptist, usually celebrated in Russia on June 23 at night. The holiday celebration is connected to the role of water in fertility and ritual purification. Youths jump over the flames of bonfires. Girls float wreaths of flowers often lit with candles on rivers and attempt to gain foresight into their relationship fortunes from the flow patterns of the flowers on the river. Men may attempt to capture the wreaths, in the hope of capturing the interest of the woman who floated the wreath (Wikipedia).

girls thought. They were looking for her the whole night and the next day and the third day, but they could not find her. Ivan and Marya were struck by grief. The old woman went to the forest every day for a long time looking for Snowmaiden, but all in vain.

Where did Snowmaiden disappear? Did a wild animal eat her? Did a huge bird take her overseas to her nest? No, it was neither an animal nor a bird's fault. When Snowmaiden ran after her friends and jumped over the fire, she melted and turned into steam, which then formed a small cloud that flew high up in the sky…

BY PERCH'S ORDERS

One old man had three sons, two smart ones and one fool – Yemelya. The elder brothers were working from morning 'til night, and Yemelya was lying on a Russian oven[5] the whole day. One winter day the two brothers went to the farmer's market, and Yemelya's sisters-in-law asked him to help them about the house. "Yemelya, please go to the river and bring some water."

He answered, "I don't want to..."

"Yemelya, get the water, or otherwise your brothers won't bring you any gifts from the market."

"All right..."

Yemelya jumped off the oven, put on his winter coat, took two buckets and an axe, and went to the river. He made an ice-hole with the axe and filled the buckets with water. When he was about to leave, he noticed a big perch in the ice-hole, so he quickly bent down and grabbed it with his hands. *The fish soup will be great,* he thought.

Suddenly the perch spoke to him in a human voice, "Yemelya, let me go, I will be of use to you."

Yemelya laughed. "How can you be useful to me? No, I will take you home to my sisters-in-law, and I will make them cook a nice fish soup."

The perch pleaded again. "Yemelya, Yemelya, please, let me go to my family and my little ones. I will do anything you want."

"All right, but first prove that you are not lying. Then I will let you go."

The perch asked him, "Yemelya, what do you want right now?"

"I want the buckets to walk home by themselves and not spill any water."

Then the perch said, "Remember my words, when you want something to happen, just say,
By perch's orders,
By my desire.
So Yemelya said,
By perch's orders,
By my desire.
Buckets, walk home yourselves!
As soon as he pronounced those words, the buckets started walking up the hill toward the village. Yemelya let the perch go back in the river and followed them. The buckets were marching along the main street, and everyone was just astonished to see them. Yemelya was walking behind them, laughing. The buckets entered the house and jumped on the bench, and Yemelya climbed back on the oven.

---

[5] A Russian oven is a unique type of oven/furnace, that first appeared in the 15th century. It is used for both cooking and house heating; it burns firewood. It is designed to retain heat for long periods of time. During the winter, people sleep atop the oven to keep warm. The Russian oven was a major element of Russian life and consequently it often appears in folklore.

Some time passed, and his sisters-in-law came up to him again with a request. "Yemelya, please chop firewood."

"I don't want to..."

"Yemelya, go chop the firewood, or otherwise your brothers won't bring you any gifts from the market."

Yemelya did not want to get off the oven and then he remembered about the perch and whispered,

By perch's orders,

By my desire

Axe, go and chop firewood, and firewood – get into the oven yourself!

The axe got out from under the bench and went outside to chop firewood, and the chopped firewood came back into the house and jumped into the oven.

Soon the sisters-in-law asked Yemelya again, "Yemelya, we don't have any more firewood. Please go to the forest and chuck some.

He replied to them from the stove, "What about you?"

"What about us?... It is not a woman's job to chuck wood."

"I don't want to..."

"Then you will not get any presents."

Yemelya sighed, climbed down from the oven, got dressed, took a rope and an axe, and went outside. Then he sat down in the sleigh and ordered his sisters-in-law, "Open the gates!"

They replied, "You fool, who gets into a sleigh without a horse?"

"I don't need a horse."

The women opened the gates, and Yemelya whispered,

By perch's orders,

By my desire

Sleigh, ride to the forest!

Right at that moment, the sleigh took off and rode so quickly that a horse-drawn sleigh would not be able to catch up. To get to the forest, Yemelya had to go through a small town first, and that's where he got into trouble. The sleigh ran over many people, and everybody started shouting, "Get him! Catch him!" He managed to escape only by a thin margin.

When he arrived in the forest he commanded,

By perch's orders,

By my desire

Axe, cut the wood, and wooden logs – get into the sleigh and tie yourselves with a rope!

Axe started to cut, and logs started to jump into the sleigh and tie themselves with a rope. When this job was done, Yemelya ordered the axe to make a big wooden butt. Then he took the axe sat into the sleigh and said,

By perch's orders,

By my desire

Sleigh, ride home!

The sleigh rushed home. On the way back, Yemelya had to go through the same small town again where the angry people were already waiting for him to return. As soon as he arrived, they grabbed him and started beating him. But Yemelya didn't lose his presence, and he whispered,

By perch's orders,
By my desire
Butt, kick them hard!

The butt came to life and started beating everyone in the crowd. The people got scared and ran away, and Yemelya continued riding home.

Time passed, and one day the Tsar himself heard about Yemelya and his tricks, so he sent an officer to bring him to the palace. The officer arrived at Yemelya's house and asked, "Are you Yemelya, the fool?"

"Why do you ask?" answered Yemelya from the top of the oven.

"Get dressed, I will take you to the Tsar."

"I don't want to..." The officer got furious and slapped him, and Yemelya responded right away,

By perch's orders,
By my desire
Butt, kick him hard!

The butt jumped out from behind the oven and started beating the officer – he barely escaped alive. The Tsar was really surprised that one of his best officers failed to accomplish his task, so he decided to send the most important nobleman to Yemelya. "Bring this fool Yemelya to me, or otherwise I will behead you!"

The nobleman went to the market and bought plenty of raisins, prunes, and cakes and then paid a visit to Yemelya's house. When he arrived, he asked the sisters-in-law what Yemelya liked.

"Our Yemelya likes when people talk nicely to him and when they promise him gifts."

The nobleman gave Yemelya raisins, prunes, and cakes and then said, "Yemelya, why are you spending all your time on top of the oven? Let's go visit the Tsar."

"I am warm and comfortable here, no need to go anywhere..."

"Yemelya, you will eat delicacies at the Tsar's palace. Please, let's go."

"I don't want to go..."

"Yemelya, the Tsar will give you wonderful gifts, a red coat, a hat, and boots."

Yemelya reflected a little bit on this offer and said, "All right. You go first, and I will follow you."

The nobleman left, and Yemelya said,

By perch's orders,
By my desire
Oven, go to the Tsar's palace!

Suddenly the corners in the house started cracking, the roof began swaying, one wall fell down, and the oven marched out of the house.

The Tsar was sitting in his palace looking out of the window when he saw an oven walking in the distance. "What is this miracle?" he asked the nobleman.

The nobleman answered, "This is Yemelya coming to see you on his oven."

The Tsar came out on the porch and asked, "Yemelya, I have received a lot of complaints about you! You ran over many people with your sleigh."

"Why did they jump under the sleigh?"

At this moment the Tsar's daughter, Marya-Tsarevna, looked out of the window. Yemelya saw her and whispered,

By perch's orders,

By my desire

Let the Tsar's daughter fall in love with me!

And then he said,

Oven, go home!

The oven turned around and walked home. It returned to its usual spot, and Yemelya kept on lying on it day after day.

Meanwhile, the Tsar's palace was turned upside down. Marya-Tsarevna was crying and yelling that she missed Yemelya, that she could not live without him and that she wanted to marry him. The Tsar asked the nobleman again to bring Yemelya back. "Bring him to me dead or alive, or I will behead you!"

The nobleman went to the market again and bought sweet wines and tasty treats and went to Yemelya's house. He organized a big feast for Yemelya, who ate and drank a lot. When Yemelya got full and drunk, he fell asleep, and the nobleman put him in his sleigh and brought him to the Tsar's palace. The Tsar immediately ordered that Yemelya and his daughter be put into a big wooden barrel, which was closed up tight and thrown into the sea.

When Yemelya woke up, he saw that he was somewhere dark and tight. *Where am I?* He wondered.

voice replied, "It is dull and dizzy here. We were put in a barrel and thrown into the sea."

"And who are you?"

"I am Marya-Tsarevna."

Yemelya ordered,

By perch's orders,

By my desire

Strong winds, get the barrel to a dry shore, on golden sand!

The winds started blowing, and the waves rose, and a big one brought the barrel to a dry shore, on golden sand. When Yemelya and Marya-Tsarevna got out of the barrel, she asked, "Yemelya, where are we going to live? Please build a small house!"

"I don't want to..."

She pleaded him some more, and he said,

By perch's orders,

By my desire
I want a palace with a gold roof to be built!

As soon as he uttered those words, a marble palace with a gold roof emerged. There was a beautiful garden around it with many flowers and birds. Marya-Tsarevna and Yemelya entered the palace and she asked again, "Yemelya, is it at all possible for you to become handsome?"

Here, Yemelya did not think long.

By perch's orders,
By my desire
I want to be handsome and fit!

And right away he became so handsome that you have never heard about such beauty even in fairy tales.

Meanwhile, the Tsar went hunting and saw a palace on the seashore where there had never been anything before. *What ignorant person dared to build a palace on my land?* he wondered. So he sent his servants to find out who was the owner. The servants came to the palace and shouted, "Who is the owner here?"

Yemelya responded, "Ask your Tsar to be my guest, I will introduce myself to him."

The Tsar went to Yemelya's palace, and Yemelya invited him to lunch. After eating plenty of delicacies, the Tsar asked, "Who are you, young man?"

"Do you remember Yemelya the Fool who came to you on an oven, and who you ordered put into a barrel with your daughter and thrown into the sea? I am that Yemelya, and I can destroy and burn all your lands and possessions, if I wish."

The Tsar got frightened and started apologizing. "Marry my daughter, Yemelya. Take all my possessions, but don't kill me, please!"

Then they threw a great feast for the whole country, and Yemelya married Marya-Tsarevna and became Tsar. At this point my tale comes to an end, and whoever listened is a brave lad.

HOT PANCAKES FOR WINTER

One very cold winter evening, a little boy, Vanya, and his mother were walking home to their village from the market. It was snowing heavily, and the chilling wind was blowing strong, and even the warmest fur coats and hats were not able to protect them from the freezing weather. In the beginning the boy was very energetic, he was skipping and singing songs, but very quickly he got cold and quiet.   Suddenly, in the middle of the road a woman appeared, wearing a long white fur coat.

"Look, mother, what a beautiful lady! Where did she come from?" Vanya asked

"Shh! This is Queen Winter herself. Don't talk, just bow to her and keep walking," his mother whispered.

"Hello! Don't pass by. Are you afraid of me? Why don't you visit me in my castle?" Winter said mockingly. She clapped her hands, and a beautiful white sleigh with a white horse emerged from the snow storm.

"Hello, Winter! I will happily be your guest," Vanya's mother answered, turning pale, "I will only take my son home to his grandmother. He is too little to pay visits so late at night."

"All right. I will wait for you here, but don't you dare cheat on me!" Winter said.

"I will be back in no time," the poor woman said, and she ran with her son toward their house.

Grandmother was waiting for them at home. Earlier that evening she had gathered the last of the flour they had and some sour cream, and she had baked one big, hot pancake. "Come in, come in, my dears! I was expecting you, and I baked this wonderful pancake for you. It is as hot as the sun, it will warm you up quickly!" grandmother said.

"It smells so good, I have never tasted such a great pancake before." Vanya said.

"Let Vanya eat, but I have to go, I promised," his mother said, and she told the grandmother how they met Queen Winter. The grandmother tried to persuade her to stay home, but the young woman only sighed and left the house.

She was walking in the snowstorm in despair. She said farewell to her son, her mother, and her house. She did not hope to see them ever again. Soon she saw Winter, who was still waiting for her. The mother was getting ready to climb into Winter's sleigh, when suddenly she heard Vanya's voice behind her back, ""Mommy, wait! Winter, wait! I brought you a hot pancake. It is not good to visit people without a gift. Winter's house is probably cold, but this pancake will warm you up," the boy said. He forgot to put his coat on and was now shivering from cold.

Winter looked at the pancake and smiled, and as she did that the wind stopped blowing, the snow stopped falling, and it got considerably warmer. "All right," Winter said, "go home, meet the spring, and have a long, happy life. It's time for me to go to the North Pole." After these words, she vanished into thin air.

"Mommy, why didn't Winter take my pancake? Was she offended by me?" asked the boy.

"No, silly!" his mother answered. "She asked you to eat it in her honor."

Vanya did not understand anything, but he ate the pancake with great pleasure. Since then there is a tradition in Russia to say farewell to Winter with big round pancakes[6] so that Winter doesn't get angry and freeze people any more.

[6] This is now a traditional yearly celebration similar to Mardi Gras called "Maslenitsa", which takes place on Sunday either the last two weeks of February or the beginning of March, 40 days before Easter.

WHY FIR TREE AND PINE TREE ARE EVERGREEN

Once upon a time, winter came too early. The leaves on the trees didn't fall yet, but it was already very cold. Small animals and reptiles hid in their burrows and dens. Migrating birds flew away to the South. All living beings either hid or left. Only one little bird stayed behind, because she had a broken wing and could not fly away with her family. She sat in an open field under a wormwood and didn't know what to do. At the end of the field, she saw a forest and decided to go there. She hoped that the trees would take pity on her and let her spend winter on their branches.

The first tree the bird saw was a beautiful birch tree. So she asked the birch, "Dear birch, your branches are so bushy. Please, let me spend winter with you."

"I have a lot of branches and a lot of leaves, and I have to take care of them all. I don't have time to take care of you," the birch tree answered.

The bird went on. Soon she saw a big oak tree. So she asked the oak, "Mighty oak, please let me spend winter on your bushy branches."

"What a silly thought," the oak answered. "If I let everybody spend winter on my branches, they will eat all my acorns. No, no, keep going!"

The bird left. When she approached the river, she saw a willow. The willow had plenty of long cozy branches, so the bird asked it, "Kind willow, your branches are so bushy and cozy. Please, let me stay with you until spring!"

"Don't interrupt me when I am having a conversation with the river. I don't talk to random strangers." the willow replied.

Poor bird with a broken wing was desperate. No one wanted to help her, and everybody looked down at her. She was walking further and further into the forest when a fir tree noticed her. "Hey, where are you going, poor fellow?" she asked the bird.

"I don't know," the bird answered.

"What do you mean, you don't know?" asked the fir tree.

"I don't know *where* to go…"

"Why didn't you fly to the South with your family?"

"I have a broken wing, I cannot fly. I came to the forest to ask trees to let me spend winter on their branches, but no one let me…"

"Oh, poor thing!" the fir tree exclaimed. "Stay with me. This branch is the warmest one – come and sit here."

An old pine tree that grew next to the fir tree overheard the conversation and pitied the little bird. "My branches are not as bushy and warm as the fir tree's, but I will use them to protect you from cold winds," the pine tree said.

The bird climbed onto the fir tree's branch, and the pine tree covered her from winter wind. Juniper that grew in between the two trees also decided to help. "Don't worry, little bird. I will feed you my berries all winter." Thus, the bird found a wonderful shelter.

One night the wind was particularly strong. He liked to play with tree leaves, tear them away, and make the branches naked. The wind enjoyed this game so much that he decided to tear off every single leaf and make all the branches naked. Before doing that, he came to ask permission from Father Frost, "Father Frost, can I make all tree branches naked?"

Father Frost answered, "You can tear the leaves off birches, willows, and others who refused to help the little bird, but don't touch those who offered protection to her. Let them be evergreen."

The wind did as Frost said and didn't touch the pine tree, the fir tree, and the juniper. Therefore, they are evergreen up to this day.

WHO IS THE STRONGEST IN THE WORLD?

An old woman lived in a small Yakut village. One winter morning she went to the river to get some water. The river was covered with ice, so she had to break the ice to make a hole to get the water. The old woman filled two buckets with water and started for home but, unfortunately, there was ice everywhere, so she slipped and fell on the ice, spilling all the water. She was very old and very slow, so while she was saying "Oh" and "Ah" and thinking how she was going to get up, the water she had spilled froze together with her skirt.

At her age, she didn't have strength to get up on her own, so she started to look around to find someone to help her. The sun was shining brightly above her, so the old woman asked, "Sun, are you the strongest in the world?"

"Yes, I am very strong, but a dark cloud can cover me."

So the old woman turned to the cloud. "Cloud, are you the strongest in the world?"

"Yes, I am very strong, but the wind can blow me away."

The old woman turned to the wind. "Wind, are you the strongest in the world?"

"Yes, I am very strong, but the mountain can block my path."

The old woman looked at the mountain and asked, "Mountain, are you the strongest in the world?"

"Yes, I am very strong, but a man can break me."

The old woman asked a young man passing by, "Young man, are you the strongest in the world?"

"Yes, I am very strong, but I am afraid of fire."

So the old woman turned to fire. "Fire, are you the strongest in the world?"

"Yes, I am very strong, but water can kill me."

The old woman turned to water. "Water, are you the strongest in the world?"

"Yes, I am very strong, but earth can drink me."

Finally, the old woman turned to earth. "Earth, are you the strongest in the world?"

"Yes, I guess I am the strongest in the world."

"Well, then let my skirt go!" said the old woman angrily. "Why are you holding it?!"

She ripped her skirt, and it separated from the ice. She got up, filled her buckets with water again, and went home to make tea for her grandsons, who already woke up.

BROWN BEAR, POLAR BEAR

One winter a long time ago, the food was very sparse, so both the polar bear and the brown bear were very hungry. Then one day the brown bear decided to leave his forest and go northwards to the sea, hoping he could get some food there. At the same time, the polar bear decided to walk on the ice southwards to the shore to see if there was some food left in the forest. They met right on the sea shore.

The polar bear saw the brown bear, and his hair stood on end. He said, "Hey, brown bear, why are you walking on my land?"

The brown bear answered, "When did you have *land*? Your place is in the sea! Your land is ice!"

The polar bear reared up, the brown bear reared up, and they started to fight. They fought 'til midday, but no one won. They fought 'til midnight, but still neither of them won. Both were very tired, so they sat down to rest quietly. The brown bear talked first, "You, polar bear, turned out to be stronger, but I am more agile and swift. This is why no one of us can win. What are we fighting for? We are brothers."

The polar bear answered, "You are right, we are brothers. We have nothing to fight for. Our territories are enormous."

The brown bear said, "Yes, my forests are huge. I have nothing to do on your ice.

The polar bear said, "I have nothing to do in your forest. I never went there! Let's live on our own territory and not disturb each other."

The brown bear returned to the forest, and the polar bear stayed on the sea shore. Since then the master of the forest lives in the forest, and the master of the sea lives in the sea, and they don't bother each other.

MASTER OF THE WINDS

Once upon a time, there was an old man who lived with his three daughters. The youngest daughter was the kindest and nicest. The family was very poor. They lived in an old chum[7] with holes in it. They didn't have many warm clothes, either. When it was too cold outside, they would sit all day around the fire. One especially severe winter, a strong snowstorm hit the tundra[8]. The wind blew for three nights and three days, and it was so strong that people started worrying that it would blow their chums away. They were afraid to go outside, so they stayed home hungry.

The old man was listening to the snowstorm carefully, and on the third day he said, "We won't survive this storm. It was sent by the Master of the Winds – Kotura. He is probably angry, and he wants us to send him a good wife. My eldest daughter, you should go to Kotura, otherwise all our people will die. Ask him to stop the snowstorm!"

"How will I go? I don't know the way." the eldest daughter answered.

"I will give you a small sleigh. Push the sleigh against the wind and follow it. The wind will untie your clothes, but you should not stop to tie them. The wind will blow snow in your boots, but you should not stop to clean them, you should not lose time. Soon you will see a tall mountain – climb it. When you get to the top, a small bird will sit on your shoulder. Be kind and gentle to her. Then sit in the sleigh and ride down the opposite side of the mountain. The sleigh will bring you to the entrance of Kotura's chum. Go in the chum but don't touch anything, just sit there and wait for him. When Kotura returns home, do everything he says."

So the eldest sister put on her coat, pushed the sleigh against the wind, and started walking behind it. Very soon the wind untied the laces on her coat, and she stopped to tie them back, having forgotten what her father had told her. Not long after that, she felt that her boots were full of snow, so she stopped to clean them. She walked a long while 'til she saw a very tall mountain. She climbed the mountain and looked around. Suddenly she saw a small bird flying toward her. The eldest daughter waved her arms and didn't let the bird sit on her shoulder, so the bird flew away. Then the girl sat on her sleigh and rode down the opposite side of the mountain. The sleigh stopped near a big chum.

The girl entered the chum and saw a lot of fried deer meat. *I am hungry. I should eat a piece or two, there is plenty here for everybody,* she thought and took a big piece of meat. When she finished eating, the skin at the chum's door moved, and a strong young man entered the chum. It was Kotura. He looked at the girl and asked, "Where did you come from? What are you doing here?"

---

[7] Chum (tent) = a nomadic tent of the Yamal-Nenets reindeer herders in Western Siberia (similar concept as tepee).

[8] Tundra = a vast area of stark landscape in the North of Russia that is frozen for much of the year. No trees grow in the tundra, only small bushes, grasses, wild flowers, and moths

My father sent me to you."

"Why would he do that?"

"He wants you to take me as your wife."

"All right, here is the meat I brought from the hunt. Boil it, then divide it into two equal parts. Leave one part here for us to eat, and put the other one on a tray and take it to a neighboring chum. Wait 'til an old woman comes out to you and takes the meat. Don't enter the chum, wait outside 'til she brings the tray back."

The girl boiled the meat, divided it into two parts, put one on a tray, and walked outside. The snowstorm was still blowing, it was dark, and she couldn't see anything. *I am not going anywhere in this weather,* she thought. She threw the meat in the snow and returned to Kotura's chum with an empty tray.

Kotura looked at her and asked, "Did you take the meat to the old lady?"

"I did."

"Show me the tray, let me see what she gave you in exchange for meat."

The girl showed him an empty tray. Kotura didn't say anything and went to sleep.

The next morning, he brought her several deer pelts and said, "I will go hunting for the day, and you will make me new clothes, mittens, and fur boots from these skins. When I come back, I will see how good a seamstress you are."

Kotura left, and the girl started working. Suddenly an elderly lady entered the chum. "Young girl," she said, "something got into my eye. Could you please help me to take it out?"

"Don't bother me, I have a lot of work to do." answered the girl. "I don't have time for this."

The old lady didn't say anything and left.

The eldest daughter continued working. She was afraid she wouldn't be able to finish everything by the evening, so she was doing everything quickly but carelessly, not paying attention to the quality of her work. It was even harder for her to make decent clothes because there were no knives or needles in Kotura's chum.

In the evening, Kotura came back from hunting and asked the girl to show him what she had accomplished. His clothes, mittens, and boots were ready, but they were hard and tight, the seams were not straight, and everything was several sizes too small. Kotura got very angry and threw the girl out of his chum into a big snowdrift, and she froze in it.

The snowstorm became even more violent. The wind was howling like a lonely wolf, and there was no end to it in sight. The old man was sitting in his old chum with two daughters, shivering from cold. He turned to his second daughter and said, "My eldest daughter didn't listen to me. She didn't do what I told her to do. This is why the snowstorm is so violent. Kotura is angry. Now you have to go to him and persuade him to stop the wind and snow."

He made his second daughter a small sleigh and explained to her everything he had told his eldest daughter. The second daughter left home. She didn't follow her father's instructions either. She cleaned her boots from snow when she felt like it, she tied her coat when the wind untied it, she was not kind to the bird on top of the tall mountain, and when she got to Kotura's chum she ate some of his meat. When Kotura came home, he asked the girl, "Why did you come here?"

"My father sent me."

"What for?"

"So that I become your wife."

"Well, boil the meat I have just brought."

When the meat was ready, Kotura gave her the same instructions he had given to her eldest sister. The girl took the meat and went looking for a neighboring chum. But the snowstorm was so strong that she couldn't see anything, so she threw away the meat and returned to Kotura, just like her eldest sister did.

"Did you take the meat to the neighboring chum?" Kotura asked.

"I did."

"What did they give you in return?"

"Nothing."

Kotura didn't say anything else and went to sleep.

The next morning, he brought several deer pelts and asked the girl to make him new winter clothes, mittens, and fur boots. After that, he went hunting again. The girl started working. Soon an old woman entered the chum and said, "Young girl, something got into my eye. Could you please help me to take it out?"

"Don't bother me, I have a lot of work to do," answered the girl. "I don't have time for you."

The old lady didn't say anything and left.

When Kotura came home in the evening, he wanted to try his new clothes on. They were rough and ugly, with uneven seams and several sizes too small. Kotura got very angry and threw the girl out of his chum into a big snowdrift, and she froze in it, too.

Meanwhile, the old man and his youngest daughter were waiting for the snowstorm to end, but it just wouldn't stop. It looked like all the chums were going to be blown off by the wind. "My daughters did not listen to me," the old man said. "They only made things worse. Kotura is now furious. You are my last daughter, but I have to send you to Kotura. If I don't do it, all our people will die from hunger."

The old man taught his youngest daughter everything he had already taught his other daughters, and the young girl left. The wind was undoing the strings on her coat, but she didn't stop to tie them. The wind blew snow in her boots, but she didn't stop to clean them. It was very cold and very hard to walk against the wind, but she just kept walking. When she climbed the tall mountain, a little bird flew toward her. The girl didn't scare the bird away but let her sit on her shoulder while she was stroking her feathers gently. When the bird flew away, the girl sat on her sleigh and rode toward Kotura's chum. When she entered the chum, she did not touch anything, just sat down and waited for him to come home.

When Kotura came home and saw the girl, he laughed. "What are you doing here?"

"My father sent me."

"What for?"

"To ask you to stop the snowstorm. Otherwise all our people will die!"

"Well, then why are you sitting here and not boiling the meat? I am hungry, and I see you haven't eaten anything either."

When the girl boiled the meat, Kotura told her to take half of it to the neighboring chum. The girl took the meat and went outside. It was dark and she couldn't see anything, not a single chum nearby, but she decided to walk at random anyway. Suddenly she saw the little bird that sat on her shoulder on top of the tall mountain. The girl decided to follow the bird, who brought her to a big tussock. It didn't look like a chum at all. The girl touched the tussock with her boot, and suddenly a door opened. An old woman came out and asked her, "Who are you? What are you doing here?"

"I brought you some meat. Kotura told me to give it to you."

"Kotura sent you? All right, give me the meat and wait here. I will be back."

Soon the old woman came out again and gave the girl her tray. The girl went back to Kotura.

"What took you so long?" Kotura asked. "Did you find the chum?"

"I did."

"Did you give the meat to the woman?"

"I did."

"Show me your tray." Kotura took the tray and saw that it was full of special knives and other instruments for making clothes from animal skins, including very good steel needles. "You've got a lot of good things here. You will make use of them tomorrow."

In the morning, Kotura brought several deer pelts and asked the girl to make him new winter clothes, mittens, and fur boots. "If you do your job well, I will make you my wife."

When Kotura left, she started working. The old woman's gifts turned out to be very handy. She gave the girl everything she needed for making clothes from animal skin. But one day was still not enough to complete this task well. Nevertheless, the girl decided not to rush and wanted to do everything properly.

Soon an old woman entered the chum. It was the same woman that the girl had met the day before. "Young girl, please help me," asked the old woman. "There is something in my eye, and I cannot take it out myself."

The girl put aside her instruments and skins and helped the woman. "Thank you," the old woman said. "My eye does not hurt any more. Now, look into my right ear."

The girl looked in her ear and got frightened.

"What did you see there?" the old woman asked.

"There is a girl in your ear!"

"Well, tell her to come out, she will help you to make clothes for Kotura."

The old man's daughter was very happy. She called the girl inside the woman's ear, and she came out… and three more with her! All four of them helped the girl to make everything Kotura asked for in no time. When the job was done, the old woman hid the four girls in her ear again and left.

In the evening, Kotura returned to his chum and asked the girl, "Did you make all the things I asked for?"

"Yes, I did."

"Let me try them on."

Kotura took the clothes from the girl, and they were nice and soft, very well made and exactly his size. Kotura smiled and said, "I like you! And my mother liked you, and my four sisters, too. You work well, and you are very brave. You were walking through a fierce snowstorm to help your people. Stay in my chum, I want you to be my wife."

And as soon as he uttered those words, the wind stopped blowing, and the snow stopped falling, and all people got warm and went out of their chums.

TWO BAGS

Once upon a time, there was a rich farmer and a poor farmer. One day the poor farmer agreed with the rich one that he would be working in his field without pay, but the rich farmer would give the poor one a quarter of his field for his own use. The poor farmer worked very hard, and a good wheat crop grew on both his and the rich farmer's part of the field. But when time came to gather wheat, Frost and hoarfrost damaged the crop on the poor man's part of the field. So it turned out that he worked the whole year for nothing.

The next year, the two farmers reached the same agreement. But this time, the poor farmer chose a different part of the field for his crop. When autumn came, the poor farmer's wheat was damaged by the frost again, and the rich farmer's wheat was intact. The poor farmer got very upset. He was hardworking and honest, but Frost deprived him of food and money for the second time. So he decided to find Frost, who killed his crop every year.

He was sharpening his axe for three days and three nights, and then he left his house and went far away to the West. Neither deer nor birds ever got that far. He went through the woods for many days and nights 'til he reached a very high mountain. He started climbing the mountain, and after three days and three nights he got to the top, where no living being had ever been before him.

On the top of the mountain there was a big house. The poor farmer entered the house and saw a long silver table with a lot of food on it. He ate some and hid under the table. Soon he heard foot steps and the Frost entered the house.

"Who ate my food?" Frost asked. "I think I smell an intruder in the house."

"Frost, I will kill you with my axe!" the poor farmer cried from under the table.

"Why do you want to kill me?" Frost asked.

"Why did you damage my crop for two years in a row but save the rich farmer's crop?" asked the poor farmer.

"My boy, I didn't know what I was freezing. Come here," said Frost.

When the poor farmer climbed from under the table, Frost offered to have dinner with him. "Don't be angry at me," said Frost. "I will give you a special gift. You will never get cold or hungry with it." So he gave him a bag. "Open this bag when you feel the need."

The poor farmer took the bag and went home. On his way home, he got very cold and hungry, so he opened the bag. Two young women came out of the bag with a lot of food, which they put in front of the poor farmer. The farmer ate enough food to last him 'til he would get to his village and continued his journey. When he returned home, he opened the bag again. Two young women came out and started throwing out all his old things, clothes, furniture, etc. Then they reached into the bag and got out all the new things that the poor farmer needed. Since then, his life was very good.

One day the rich farmer paid him a visit. He was surprised that the poor farmer was not asking permission to work in his field any more. "Where did you get all these riches?" he asked in astonishment.

"Am I supposed to be poor all my life?" the poor farmer answered proudly.

The rich farmer became very jealous and decided to find out his secret. He invited the poor farmer to his house and made him eat a lot of food and drink a lot of strong wine. When the poor farmer got drunk, he told the story about the magical bag Frost had given him. When the rich farmer and his wife learned about the bag, they gave the poor farmer even more wine. When he got very drunk, they made him sell the bag.

That's how the poor farmer lost his treasure. He had to lead his poor life again, being cold and hungry almost every day. He cried for a long time because of his stupidity and then decided to visit Frost again. He took his axe and went westward through the forests to the big mountain. He climbed the mountain, entered Frost's house, and sat down at the table to wait for him. When Frost came back home the farmer said, "You were freezing my crop for two years, and now you still make me cold and hungry every day."

"My friend, I gave you a magical thing that was supposed to help you all your life," answered Frost.

"The rich man tricked me and got my bag. Kill me or save me!" the poor farmer said.

Frost went into his closet and brought another bag, which was bigger and more beautiful than the first one. "Give this bag to the rich guy and take yours back," he said.

So the poor farmer went home with another bag. Halfway through his journey, he got hungry, so he opened the bag. Two big men jumped out of the bag and started beating him. The poor farmer closed the bag quickly and rushed home.

When he went back to his village, he went straight to the rich farmer's house. "Look, I have got another bag. It is bigger and more beautiful than the first one," said the poor farmer.

The rich farmer liked the bag very much and told the poor farmer, "I will trade you. Here is your old bag, give me this new one."

The poor farmer took his old bag and went home. The rich farmer decided to invite all his rich friends to dinner to show them that he had become the richest of all. When all the guests arrived, he opened the bag and said, "Look what I've got!"

Two big men jumped out of the bag and started beating all the rich guys. Everybody ran away from the greedy farmer's house, screaming. As for the poor farmer, he lived happily ever after.

THE OWL AND THE RAVEN

A long time ago, there were two friends, the owl and the raven. They were both white, and they really didn't like it because they were pale and unattractive and no one could distinguish them from the snow.

Once the raven came to the owl and said, "We are both white and ugly. Let's color each other."

The owl replied, "This is a good idea, let's do it."

The raven was very happy and said, "Excellent! Go ahead and color my back."

The owl answered, "It was your idea, so you color me first, and then I will color you."

"All right, let me color you first," the raven said.

He took some black oil from an oil lamp and a feather from his tail and began decorating the owl. He colored very carefully. He drew small grey dots on the owl's back and front and bigger dots on her wings. When he was finished he said, "I made you so beautiful, owl. Look at yourself!"

The owl looked at her wings, her front, and her back and was very pleased. "Indeed, I look very pretty. Now it's your turn, raven. I will make you very handsome."

The raven turned his back to her and closed his eyes in anticipation. The owl did a great job, too. She drew lovely patterns on the raven's feathers, and when she finished coloring she suddenly realized that she'd made the raven even more gorgeous than she was. The owl became very jealous, so she took the remaining black oil and spilled it on the raven's head. In a second the raven turned all black, and the owl flew away.

When the raven opened his eyes, he saw that he was all plain black. He was very upset and started crying. Since then, the owls are white with grey dots on their feathers, and the ravens are black, and owls and ravens are not friends any more.

TWO GIFTS

Once upon a time, two neighbors lived in a small village, Ahsar and Aslan. Ahsar was a kind and very hardworking man. He worked from early morning 'til late evening, and if anybody asked him for help, he never turned his back on a person.

Aslan was a greedy, calculating, and sly man. He didn't like to work and was always trying to find a way to make others work for him. He was constantly dreaming of becoming rich. He used to come to Ahsar and ask him to help with bringing firewood from the forest or repairing the roof or something else. He knew that Ahsar would never refuse, he would postpone his work and always help a neighbor. That's how they lived for many years until one extraordinary event happened.

One cold winter day, Ahsar went to the forest to get some firewood. On his way back home, he suddenly heard a bird chirping weakly in the bushes. He looked carefully and saw a small swallow with a broken wing, shivering from cold. Ahsar put it in the pocket of his winter coat and said, "Let the one who broke your wing never be happy! You should be with your family now, somewhere warm." He brought the bird home, gave it some food and water, and said, "Don't worry, you will be safe here. And in spring you will fly wherever you want."

The whole winter, Ahsar and his wife were taking care of the swallow as if it was their child, and by spring it completely recovered. When migrating birds came back from the South, Ahsar took the bird outside and let her go. It flew in a circle over his head confidently and then started making a nest under his roof. Ahsar and his wife were watching the bird and the chicks all summer, and they couldn't have been any happier.

In autumn the swallow flew away with other birds, but not without tweeting loudly and cheerfully just before she took off. The whole next winter, Ahsar and his wife were thinking about the bird. They were wondering whether it was safe and sound and whether it would come back next spring and remember them…

The swallow did not forget them. As soon as the days became warm, it came back to its nest. Ahsar and his wife heard the chirping under their roof and rushed outside. They were very happy. "How wonderful! Our bird didn't forget us."

The bird approached them and dropped a seed on the ground. It was a very unusual seed they had never seen before, so Ahsar and his wife decided to plant it to see what would grow out of it.

Soon a little plant showed up, then it grew taller and got big leaves. After that a marvelous flower blossomed, which eventually turned into a round pumpkin. The pumpkin was small at first, but by the harvest time it became huge. People from the whole village came to Ashar's garden to look at this enormous pumpkin. Aslan also stopped by and asked, "Neighbor, give me the seeds of this pumpkin so that I can grow the same ones in my garden, too."

When the pumpkin got ripe, Ashar and his wife could barely roll it in their shed – it was so heavy. Ashar wanted to open it with a knife, but the knife bent. Then he brought an axe, but the axe got broken. *What should I do with it if I cannot open it?* Ahsar thought.

Suddenly the extraordinary pumpkin opened by itself, and hundreds of gold coins poured out of it. Everyone who saw that miracle was astonished. For a week the villagers didn't talk about anything but the magic pumpkin. When Aslan heard that story, he turned green from jealousy. He hurried to Ahsar's house and started to question him about where he got the magic seeds. Ahsar was an honest person, so he told Aslan the truth about the swallow.

Early the next morning, Aslan ran to the forest to look for swallows. It was a couple of weeks before winter, so not all of them had left yet. When he saw several birds sitting on a branch of a tree, he took a big stone and threw it at them. The stone hit one swallow and broke a wing. Aslan grabbed it and brought it home. The whole winter he fed the bird but kept it in a box so that it did not fly away. By spring its wing healed, and Aslan took it outside. The swallow took off and flew toward the forest.

Summer, autumn, and winter passed, but Aslan didn't see the swallow again. He kept wondering if it was worth a bother. When spring came, Aslan would go outside every day to look at the sky, waiting for the bird to come back with a gift. He nearly broke his neck staring up at the clouds all the time.

One day the swallow returned and dropped Aslan a seed. He was very excited. He ran to his garden and planted the seed right away. All days and nights Aslan was patrolling the garden so that no one would steal his seed, and when the pumpkin emerged he brought his bed to the garden and slept next to it. The pumpkin was growing fast, and Aslan would stare at it in adoration and whisper, "Grow bigger, bigger! Two, three times bigger than Ahsar's!"

In the middle of autumn, the pumpkin turned yellow and looked very ripe. One night Aslan decided to pick it up so that no one would see him. He called his laborers and asked them to take the pumpkin into his house. Then he sent everybody away and locked the entrance door. *It will be better this way,* he thought. *People in the village will not be able to find out how much money I have got.* He also checked that his wife was sound asleep. He didn't want anyone to disturb him. He locked himself with the pumpkin in the kitchen and waited for it to open up. *I will be very rich soon, richer than Ahsar. I will not give away a single coin.* he thought, rubbing his hands.

Then, in the middle of the night, the pumpkin cracked in the middle and started opening up. But instead of gold coins, black snakes started pouring out, hundreds of them! They all jumped on greedy Aslan and started biting him. Aslan started crying for help, but no one heard him…

As for Ahsar, he lived a long and happy life with his wife, helping villagers in need.

SUN, RAVEN, AND DAUGHTER OF THE NORTH

Once upon a time, there were two friends who lived in the tundra, Sun and Raven. Both were strong and daring, and the whole tundra knew about their bravery. Nobody could say who was the better of the two.

Many times Sun heard from Wind that North had a very beautiful daughter, and many courageous men tried to reach North's house to see his daughter, but no one came back alive. Sun thought, *I am the strongest in the world. I turn ice into water, and tundra snowy deserts start flowering when my warm rays touch the ground. I cannot believe that I will not be able to melt the frosts that North created to shield himself and his daughter.* So he dressed well in two fur coats made from deer pelts, got into his sled pulled by reindeer, and took off northward.

The longer he traveled, the colder it got. Soon Sun started noticing dog and reindeer bones on the ground and then human bones, too. The wind was blowing, the frost was biting, and the ground was cracking. Sun got frostbites on his fingers and toes, the reindeer could hardly breathe, and there was still no North's house in sight. So Sun decided to turn around and go home. On his way back, he also got a frostbite on his nose, but he was happy to return alive.

One day Sun went to gather firewood and met his friend, Raven, and his younger brother who came out for the same reason. Raven's brother asked, "Who is that?"

"It is Sun," answered Raven.

"It's so funny – Sun without a nose!" the little boy laughed.

"Shh, Sun will hear you, and he will get very angry," said Raven.

Sun overheard their conversation and said, "Don't laugh! I warm the whole Earth, and even I got my cheeks and nose frostbitten. What will happen to you when you go where I have been?"

Then Raven asked, "Where have you been, Sun?"

Sun told them the story about North and his daughter. Many young men died searching for her, and no one ever saw her.

"So this is not a fairy tale," said Raven, who had heard this story before. "So how does one get to North's house?"

"You have to go that direction where the northerly winds blow from," Sun answered.

This story kept lingering in Raven's mind and he thought, *I am young and strong. I am flying above the clouds. I can also dive deep into the sea. I've been on top of mountains and on the bottom of the ocean. I cannot believe I am not able to reach the North's house!* He went to ask his wise father for advice. "Tell me, father, how can I get to the North?"

"There is only an icy desert there, my son," the old Raven answered.

"It's not true. Powerful North and his beautiful daughter live there. Many strong men tried to find them, but all of them failed. I will not be able to sleep if you don't tell me everything you know about the North!"

"All right, my son, since you already know that it is not a fairy tale, this is what I can tell you. Your grandfather died on his way to the North. Our regular clothes are not suitable for that journey. You have to go to the bottom of the sea where your real father lives. He is the Master of the Seas. He could not bring you up in the sea, so he gave you to me when you were a little boy. Tell him you are his son, and he will help you to get to the North."

Raven dove to the bottom of the sea and went to his father's chum. The Master of the Seas was very happy to see him and asked, "How can I help you?"

"Father" Raven said, "I need to get to the North."

"Aha, you want to get to the North's house and take his daughter! 'Til now, no one has succeeded in this endeavor. I will give you stone reindeers. They don't need food, and they don't get cold. You will ride on them without a stop, and you can leave them wherever you want because nobody will take them – they look just like stones. But most important, I will give you a seal. You will have to put the seal on when you hear the sound of the ceremonial drum. When you come to the North's house, don't tell him who you really are. Tell him you are his nephew Seal. There will be a strong snow storm in the North's house, but don't pay attention to it, and don't ask him about his daughter – he hates grooms. You will see a big vase made of ice on one of the walls. In the evenings, North's sons hit the vase with sticks, and it produces wonderful sounds. Take a straw from your insole and hit the bottom of the vase several times – the vase will break. Then follow your instincts. Don't try to take North's daughter with you right away, you will not succeed. Come back, and I will give you other advice how to get her. For now, just try to get to the North. Good luck!"

Raven left. He rode a day and a night without rest. The frost was getting stronger, the snowstorm was howling, and the ground was cracking. Bones were covering the ground all along the way. Raven got frostbite on his toes, fingers, and nose, and he started to think about turning back when suddenly he heard a weak sound of a ceremonial drum. At first he thought that his ears were ringing, but then the sound got stronger. He took a knife and started to cut his regular clothes. It was very hard to do because of frostbite, but he finally managed to take off his clothes and put the seal on. He got warm right away. Now wind and snow were flying by but were not touching him.

North came out of his chum and saw a black dot approaching. He sent the strongest winds in that direction, but the dot was still moving and getting closer. He told his wife, "Look, somebody is coming. Usually when I blow hard everyone freezes, but this one keeps moving. Who could it be?"

North's youngest son peered into the snowstorm and said, "It is Seal!"

Very soon Raven-Seal reached North's chum.

"Hello, my guest," North said.

"Hello!"

"Why did you come here?"

"Just visiting. My mother is your sister. She sent me to see how you are doing."

"Well, come inside."

Raven entered the chum and sat on white animal skins. On one of the walls he saw a huge ice vase. North's sons started hitting the vase with sticks and dancing to the beautiful sounds it produced. Raven took a straw and hit the bottom of the vase. The bottom fell off, and a stunningly beautiful girl fell out of it. *Now I understand why everybody was trying to get here,* Raven thought. *North got a real treasure.* Raven continued to hit the vase with a straw, pretending not to see anything.

North thought, *Maybe the guest doesn't really see well.* So he pretended to go to sleep.

Raven also pretended to go to sleep. When he closed his eyes, North grabbed his daughter and took her to another chum. After that, everybody was sound asleep.

Early in the morning, when North and his family were still sleeping, Raven sneaked out to another chum. When he entered, North's daughter was sitting on the skins waiting for him.

"Are you Raven?" she asked.

"Yes, you are right."

"I was waiting for you. I knew you were coming. I got fed up sitting in an ice vase or in this chum. My father does not even let me go out to look at the sun, I have never seen it."

"It's good you haven't seen Sun." Raven thought about his rival. Then he said, "You are very beautiful. I have never seen girls like you. Tomorrow I will go home, but if you want, I will come back on my stone reindeers and take you with me to my people."

"Yes, please come back!" the girl answered.

Raven put the seal back on and left the chum. After that he took his sled and went hunting. He killed several reindeer and brought them to North in the evening. "Look uncle, here are my gifts to you. Tomorrow I will go home, but soon I will come back, since I already know the way here."

North thought, *What should I do with him? If he got here the first time, he will get here the second time, too.* "All right, nephew, come back," North said.

The next morning, Raven left North's chum. He went straight to the bottom of the sea to his father.

"Well, my son, tell me about your adventures. Did you reach the North? Did you see his daughter?"

"Yes, I got there and saw her. She agreed to be my wife. I did not take her with me, as you had advised me," Raven answered.

"You did good, very good. Now, take the herds of whales, sea lions, walruses, and seals and drive them to the North. When the animals start moving the water will rise and create a big wave. It will help you."

North was sitting in his chum drinking hot tea when his youngest son rushed in and cried, "Father, look! A huge wall of water is moving our way!"

North looked outside and thought, *Wow, it may drown everything!* Then he ordered his sons, "Run to the top of the highest mountain!"

Everyone rushed to the highest mountain and forgot North's daughter in the ice vase. Raven arrived with the wave and ran straight to North's chum and grabbed the vase with the girl. Then he shouted to North, "Hey, North, I fulfilled my promise. I came back. Why did you climb that mountain?"

"Where is my daughter?" North asked his wife.

"We forgot her at home in the ice vase…" she answered.

Raven raised his hand, and the water subsided and retreated. The herds of whales, sea lions, walruses, and seals remained on the shore next to North's chum. North and his family returned home, and Raven held his daughter and said, "I am not Seal. I am Raven, the son of the Master of the Seas. You have just seen my powers, but I am not taking your daughter by force. This is her wish."

"Yes, father, I want to leave with Raven. I am tired of sitting in an ice vase, I want to see the world," the girl said.

"Fine," North said,. "I only ask you to let her go if and when she wants to come back home."

"All right, "Raven said, "I will do so. And now take all these animals as my gift to you," and he pointed to the herds of whales, sea lions, walruses, and seals. He wrapped North's daughter in furs, and they left in his sled.

When Sun learned that Raven returned from the North, he came to him and asked, "I heard you visited North?"

"Yes, I did."

"Did you see his daughter?"

"Not only did I see her, I married her!"

"Show her to me."

"Here, look," Raven said while entering his chum. An amazingly beautiful young woman was sitting inside. It was North's daughter.

When Sun saw her he said, "Give her to me! We are friends, almost brothers, and you know the tradition of our ancestors, my friend's wife can be my wife."

"No, I will never give her up!" Raven answered firmly.

Sun got angry and left the tundra. Day turned into night, and night became long. People in the tundra got scared that they would never see the sun again, and they came to Raven to ask him not to anger Sun. Raven sent a woman to Sun, but she returned soon and said, "Sun didn't even look at me."

Then Raven sent Sun his sister, who was very beautiful, too. She came to Sun and pleaded, "Come back to us, give us back daylight! If you want, I will be your wife."

"No, let Raven give me the daughter of the North first, then I will return to the tundra."

"Am I worse than her?" the beauty asked.

"Fine. You are not as beautiful as her, but I will marry you. However, we will never go back to the tundra. Raven must know that he shouldn't have offended his mighty friend," Sun said.

"Do you think I can be happy away from my family?" the girl asked.

"All right, we will live a little bit here and a little bit in the tundra. People of the tundra will see me again, but not for a long while. Let Raven remember this."

As for the daughter of the North, she saw that people of the tundra were cold and unhappy, and Raven was not powerful enough to bring Sun to the tundra. She laughed at him and went back home to live with her father North. Since then, the sun lives far away overseas and sends only his coldest rays to the tundra.

PSIA information can be obtained at www.ICGtesting.com
inted in the USA
VIW12n0232021216
9578BV00009B/46